By Lisa Banim

Based on the television series, "Lizzie McGuire", created by Terri Minsky

New York

"Miranda, what's wrong?" Lizzie McGuire asked as her best friend sank into the seat next to her. "Why is your face all scrunched up like that?"

Miranda Sanchez slumped back in the school bus seat and crossed her arms. "I'm not scrunching," she said. "I'm *squinting*. I think I'm going blind."

"Your eyesight was twenty-twenty on those eye chart tests we had in the nurse's office last week," David Gordon, Lizzie's other best friend, chimed in from across the aisle. "That's a perfect score."

"Not regular blind, Gordo," Miranda said. "*Color* blind. I'm seeing everything in blue and white."

"Actually, color blindness means a person sees in black and white," Gordo argued. "Or more accurately, shades of—"

Um, hello. More than I needed to know, Gordo.

"You're not seeing things," Lizzie assured Miranda quickly. "Everyone on the bus is wearing blue and white, except you." She pointed to her own blue and white hoodie and jeans. "It's School Spirit Day, remember?"

"By official decree of the Queen of Mean, Kate Sanders," Gordo added. He lifted up one foot to show his school spirit. "See? Blue sock. The other one's white."

"You wore mismatched socks on purpose?" Miranda said, lifting one eyebrow.

Gordo shrugged. "And don't forget about the big pep rally this afternoon in the gym," he added. "Everyone has to go. And we have to be . . . peppy."

> Hey, I can do peppy! My middle name is Peppy! See? See?

"Well, I don't think School Spirit Day is so bad," Lizzie said. "Maybe it will help get our football team psyched for the big game on Saturday."

Just then, the bus stopped and a tall, tanned, blond girl dressed head to toe in Hillridge colors bounded up the stairs. "Hey, y'all!" she called as she waved to everyone on the bus. "Happy School Spirit Day!"

"This day just keeps getting worse," Miranda muttered.

Lizzie had to agree with her friend. Tammy Jean Honeycutt had moved to Hillridge from Texas a month ago, but she was already driving Lizzie and Miranda crazy.

Tammy Jean was just so nice all the time. Too nice.

To Lizzie's horror, the new girl sat right in front of them, next to a tall, skinny boy named Martin Oglethorpe.

Martin didn't look horrified, though. And neither did Gordo. In fact, both of them were smiling at Tammy Jean. All the guys at school liked her.

It was sickening.

"Isn't it a bee-yoo-tiful day?" Tammy Jean said, twisting around in her seat to face Lizzie and Miranda. Even her eye makeup was in Hillridge colors. She had a blue-and-white daisy painted on her cheek, too. "Just perfect for—"

Suddenly, Tammy Jean stopped. Her mouth dropped open. "Omigosh," she said. "Miranda, you're not wearing spirit colors!"

"Yeah," Miranda said. "I forgot."

"Well, that just won't do," Tammy Jean said, sounding very concerned. She rummaged in her blue-and-white backpack and pulled out some extra hair accessories and face paint. "I can fix you right up."

Uh-oh, Lizzie thought. I'd better do something before Miranda gets mad. "So, Tammy Jean," Lizzie said brightly, trying to distract the blond girl. "How do you like being on the Hillridge cheer squad?"

"Oh, I love it," Tammy Jean said. "Did you know that I was head cheerleader back at my old school in Austin? We were state cheer champs three times in a row. Our team's name was the Aardvarks."

"How can we forget?" Miranda muttered. "You've only told us about a zillion times."

"Fascinating," Gordo said, mesmerized.

So she's gorgeous and has a cute Southern drawl. Big deal.

"With three championships, I guess it must be a big step down for you to cheer for Hillridge," Miranda said.

A few rows ahead of them, Kate Sanders's head snapped around. "Excuuuuse me, Sanchez?" she said.

Lizzie slumped a little in her seat. Kate, her former best friend from fourth grade, was super-popular. She was also head cheerleader of the Hillridge squad. It wasn't a good idea to mess with her.

But Tammy Jean turned toward Kate with a huge smile. "Oh, I just loooved cheering at my first Hillridge game last week. And guess what? I told Ms. Bailey, the faculty cheerleading adviser, that I'd be happy to give all the girls some tips. Why, I'll have the squad at championship level in no time."

Kate dug her long, blue-and-white fingernails into the back of the bus seat. "Oh, really?" she said. "Let me give you a majorly helpful piece of 411, Ms. Ex-Texas. The head cheerleader job at Hillridge is taken. Permanently. By ME."

Tammy Jean smiled again. "Well now, we'll just have to see about that, won't we?" she said sweetly.

Lizzie glanced at Kate. For once, the Duchess of Diss seemed speechless.

"Let the games begin," Gordo said in a low voice to Lizzie and Miranda. "This is one pep rally that might actually be fun!"

"What did you say about *fun*, Gordo?" Miranda asked as the three friends sat in the bleachers in the gym. "This is the most boring pep rally ever."

"Miranda," Lizzie said. "It hasn't even started yet."

All around them, kids were still filing into the bleachers. Blue-and-white streamers and balloons were everywhere. The Hillridge Junior High marching band was warming up right in front of Lizzie and her friends.

"Okay, then," Gordo said. "If you were stuck on a desert island, what three DVDs would you take with you?"

"None, because there aren't any DVD players on a desert island," Lizzie pointed out.

Gordo shrugged. "Just trying to make conversation."

Miranda sniffed the air. "Something really reeks in here," she said. "Whatever it is, I'm not bringing it to that desert island."

"Ewww," Lizzie agreed, wrinkling her nose. "What is that?"

"It's probably coming from the cafeteria," Gordo said. "The Tuna Slop Surprise at lunch was pretty lethal."

"Wait, I know!" Miranda said. "Somebody's wearing that gross-o Team Spirit cologne. Someone spilled some when I was at the mall last week and it made me gag. Big-time."

Principal Tweedy strode out to the middle of the gym floor and motioned for quiet. "Good afternoon, students," he said into a microphone. "Welcome to our first Hillridge Junior High pep rally of the year, organized by Kate Sanders. In just a few moments, our very own Hillridge cheer squad will lead us all in a rousing—"

Blah, blah, blah.

"If you ask me," Gordo said to Lizzie and Miranda in a low voice, "forcing kids to exhibit pep against their will is a very dubious endeavor."

Martin Oglethorpe, the geeky guy from the bus, turned around. "Hey, lighten up, Gordon. We get out of class, don't we? Wouldn't you rather watch a bunch of girls cheerleading than Mr. Pettus mixing combustible chemicals?"

Martin looked eagerly toward the door to the girls' locker room that the cheer queens would run through any second. "Especially Tammy Jean Honeycutt. What a babe."

"Guess he's gotten over that major crush he had on Kate last spring," Miranda muttered to Lizzie.

"Well, I think Kate let him know she wasn't exactly interested," Lizzie whispered back. "Remember how she got some of the guys on the team to hide Martin's tuba in the locker room shower?"

"Oh, yeah," Miranda said, giggling. "They filled it with bubbles."

That was pretty low. But what do you expect from the Queen of Mean?

"You have to feel sorry for poor Martin," Lizzie said.

Miranda punched at a blue-and-white beach ball that was being tossed around the bleachers.

"Tammy Jean . . . Kate Sanders . . . the guy clearly has no taste."

Just then the girls' locker room door burst open. The Hillridge cheerleaders ran out onto the gym floor in a blur of blue and white.

Martin tooted out a "Ta-da, ta-daaa!" charge on his tuba.

"Ouch," Gordo said, holding his hands over his ears.

Lizzie frowned. "What's all that white stuff floating behind the cheer queens? It's like some weird cloud that followed them out of the dressing room."

"Sugar substitute?" Miranda answered.

"Athlete's foot powder?" Gordo offered.

Lizzie rolled her eyes. "No, guys, I'm serious." She pointed down at the strange white mist that was drifting toward the cheerleaders. "In a minute, it'll be hard to see the squad."

"Just the way we like it," Miranda said, matter-of-factly.

Kate started the first cheer: "Eenie meenie minie mo! Catch those Jaguars by the toe!" she yelled.

Suddenly, Tammy Jean jumped in and waved away the mist with a sneeze. "If they holler, don't let go!" she shouted over Kate. "Eenie meenie, Hillridge, GO!!"

All of the cheerleaders lined up behind Tammy Jean. They shook their pom-poms and joined in: "GOOO, Wildcats!!!"

Lizzie saw Kate glare at Tammy Jean as the white cloud got bigger. Then the head cheer queen began to cough and sneeze.

Kate wiped her eyes with the arm of her Hillridge sweater.

"I don't believe it," Miranda said in awe. "Kate's actually crying."

"Kate doesn't cry," Lizzie said. "That white stuff probably just got in her eyes."

Tammy Jean stepped in front of Kate and started the next cheer. "That's all right, that's okay, who's gonna win on Saturday?" she called.

"Hillridge!" all the students in the bleachers screamed.

Tammy Jean kept cheering. All the other cheer queens fell in beside her. They were starting to cough and sneeze now, too.

"Give me an H!" Tammy Jean cried.

"H!" everyone shouted.

"H-I-!" Tammy Jean called.

"H-I!" the students cheered.

"Incredible," Gordo said.

Martin Oglethorpe turned around. "I agree," he said. "Isn't that Tammy Jean unbelievable?"

Ms. Bailey, the cheerleading adviser, also seemed totally impressed. Even Lizzie had to admit that Tammy Jean was doing a great job.

But Kate looked like she was about to erupt. Her face was purple through the white dust. Lizzie gasped as the head cheer queen stuck out a sneaker and tried to trip Tammy Jean!

Luckily, Tammy Jean was much too quick for Kate. She stepped aside nimbly.

Just then, Kate sneezed again and lost her balance. She hit the gym floor like a ton of bricks. As she went down, she fell into one of the cheerleaders next to her. Then they all fell like dominoes, except Tammy Jean, who had been standing in front of everyone.

"Now *that's* what I call a pyramid," Gordo said, clapping.

Lizzie stood up to get a better view. "I hope they're all okay," she said. "That must have hurt."

Tammy Jean ran toward the group and pulled each girl up, one by one. "Let's hear it for our Hillridge Wildcats cheerleaders!" she called, sneezing.

All of the cheerleaders lined up and tried to smile. As they began to jump around and shake their blue-and-white pom-poms, another dust cloud started to form.

"Ker-CHOO!" Tammy Jean sneezed through a megaphone.

Then, all of the cheerleaders started sneezing uncontrollably.

Someone sitting near Lizzie and her friends snickered.

Then the whole crowd began to laugh.

"Omigosh!" Lizzie said. "That white cloud around the cheer queens isn't dust. It's sneezing powder!"

"Lizzie, what do you think we should do?"
Miranda asked. "This place is getting crazy!"

Lizzie looked around. The Hillridge Junior
High gym was in total chaos.

Down on the floor, the cheerleaders were still
sneezing. Ms. Bailey, the squad adviser, was busy
trying to wave away the dust and hustle the girls
toward the locker room.

Tammy Jean was still trying to cheer.

Principal Tweedy was marching toward the
microphone.

Some kids in the crowd were laughing and hooting, but others were starting to sneeze as the cloud drifted up toward the bleachers.

Gordo shook his head. "I think this pep rally can now be officially classified as a total disaster," he said.

In front of them, Martin Oglethorpe grabbed his tuba and began pushing his way to the gym floor. "Never fear, Martin's here!" he called to the cheerleaders.

"It's Super Dweeb to the rescue!" Miranda said quietly. "We're saved!"

"Miranda," Lizzie said. "He's just trying to help. I'm going down there, too."

When she got to the gym floor, Martin was standing with the cheerleaders. "Allow me to offer my assistance to you ladies," she heard him say.

Lizzie cringed. Miranda was right. The kid was Super Dweeb.

Kate looked furious. "If you really want to

help, Oglethorpe, why don't you make yourself scarce and get us all some tissues?" she said as she glared at him. Then she wiped her eyes with her sweater again.

Amazing. Even when she's crying, Kate can give the evil eye.

Martin nodded like a puppy and ran toward the boys' locker room.

"Shall we start a new cheer?" Tammy Jean asked the remaining cheerleaders.

Not a good idea, Lizzie thought. The cheer queens all looked a little . . . unglued, even Claire, Kate's current best friend.

"Hey, y'all!" Tammy Jean called into the bleachers. "You got the spirit? Let's hear it!"

But the only answer from the crowd was a roar of laughter.

"Oh, dear," Ms. Bailey said. "Tammy Jean,

you've showed some wonderful spirit and leadership today. But I don't think we should continue—"

"Hey, let's hear it for the Sneeze Queens!" someone called from the bleachers.

Everyone started laughing again.

Tammy Jean finally gave up and ran from the gym in tears.

Holding their noses to keep from breathing in the dust, the other cheer queens followed Tammy Jean. All except Kate, who glared at the crowd before stomping off.

Miranda and Gordo came down the bleacher stairs and stood next to Lizzie.

"You know, I actually feel really sorry for the cheerleaders," Lizzie said. "Someone put that sneezing powder on their pom-poms. On purpose. And I'm going to find out who."

"Lizzie," Miranda said, "every one of those cheer queens has been mean or snobby to part of the Hillridge student body at one point or another."

"Yeah. Maybe they deserve a little payback," Gordo said.

"I know, but still . . ." Lizzie's voice trailed off as she noticed a red-haired girl standing by the door. She had a baseball cap pulled down low over her face,

Who *is* that girl? Lizzie wondered.

She looked strangely familiar, all right, but Lizzie couldn't quite place her. Maybe she was in one of her classes.

Whoever she was, the red-haired girl seemed to have enjoyed the sneeze show. She was smiling broadly.

Just then, the lights in the gym went out. A message blinked onto the scoreboard overhead. It said:

2, 4, 6, 8
WHY DON'T YOU
JUST GO HOME
KATE?

Then the message disappeared—and a picture of Kate flashed on the scoreboard.

It was not a very flattering photograph. Kate was sneering even more than usual.

Uh-oh, Lizzie thought. Good thing she's not here to see this.

The lights quickly came on again. By this time Principal Tweedy had finally managed to take control of the situation.

"Boys and girls!" he shouted into the microphone. "This pep rally is OVER!"

The students in the crowd began to cheer. For real this time.

"I expect to see you all at the big game against the Jefferson Jaguars on Saturday," the principal added. "On your very best behavior. Or there WILL be consequences. Please go to your next class."

"You were right, Gordo. This pep rally actually was fun," Miranda said as they walked out of the gym.

Just then, Martin ran past them into the gym. His arms were filled with rolls of paper towels from the boys' locker room. "Tammy Jean! I've got them!" he shouted.

"You're a little too late," Gordo called after him.

"So much for Super Dweeb," Miranda said. Lizzie frowned at her friend.

"I'm heading to my locker, okay?" Gordo told them. "I need to pick up my camera for photography club."

"No prob," Lizzie said. "We'll catch you later."

As Gordo hurried off, an arm reached out from the cheerleaders' equipment closet—and pulled Lizzie and Miranda inside!

"Hey!" Lizzie protested from inside the dark equipment closet. "Let go of me!"

"Yeah, what do you think you're doing?" Miranda demanded. "Whoever you are."

"Shh!" a voice told them. "Someone will hear you."

Lizzie would know that voice anywhere. She fumbled for the light switch next to the door and flipped it on.

Sure enough, Kate was standing behind Lizzie and Miranda. Her eyes were red and swollen and a river of black mascara was running down her face.

The scary, puffy monster lurking within Kate Sanders has finally been revealed. Eek!!!

Miranda rubbed her shoulder. "Did you have to dig your talons into me?" she asked Kate.

"Shh!" Kate said again. She opened the door and carefully peeked right and left down the hallway.

"Stop shushing us," Miranda said loudly. "Or—"

"Okay, okay," Kate said. "I'm sorry I had to drag you in here. But I couldn't risk having anyone see me talking to geeks."

"Gee, thanks," Lizzie told her.

"Actually, I don't want anyone to see me at all," Kate said. "I'm the laughingstock of the whole school. I just can't believe how two-faced everyone is. How dare they laugh at me? I'm the most popular girl in the eighth grade!"

Not to mention the snobbiest, Lizzie said to herself. She sighed. "What do you want, Kate?"

"You have to help me," Kate said.

"No way," Miranda told her.

Kate crossed her arms. "Okay," she said. "I need your help."

"Nope," Miranda replied cheerfully.

"Okay, fine!" Kate threw up her hands. "I'm asking for your help. Practically begging. I've had a very bad day today, in case you didn't notice."

"Yeah," Lizzie said. "We noticed. Sorry about the pep rally."

Kate dabbed at her nose with a wadded-up tissue. "Here's the deal, McGuire. You're pretty good at solving mysteries. I remember how you found my teddy bear, Mr. Stewart Wugglesby, back in grade school."

"True," Lizzie said. Miranda rolled her eyes.

"You've also solved a few cases around school lately," Kate went on.

Just call me Lizzie "Sherlock" McGuire.

"Also true," Lizzie said, nodding.

"So I want you to find out who ruined my pep rally," Kate said.

Miranda nudged Lizzie and gave her a look that said, "No! No! No!"

"The sneezing powder was probably just someone playing a joke," Lizzie told Kate. "You know, a one-time deal."

"Well, it wasn't funny," Kate said. "And I know I was the target, not the whole cheerleading squad."

Yes, Kate. Because the whole world revolves around you.

Then Lizzie remembered the awful picture of Kate on the scoreboard. Maybe she did have a point.

I hate it when that happens.

"Someone just wanted the pep rally to look bad so I, as head cheerleader, would look stupid," Kate said.

"Gee, who would want to do that?" Miranda asked. She tapped her chin, pretending to think hard.

Kate ignored her. She reached down and pulled a crumpled piece of paper from her sneaker. "Here," she said to Lizzie. "Check this out."

Lizzie unfolded the paper. In hot-pink sparkle marker, it said:

KATE: DO THE HILLRIDGE WILDCATS A FAVOR AND SPLIT

Lizzie gulped. That didn't sound good at all.

Miranda peered over her shoulder. "Hey, that's pretty clever," she said. "Split. Like cheerleaders do splits. Get it?"

This time, Kate glared at Miranda. Then she turned back to Lizzie. "I found it in my locker before the pep rally," she said.

"Did you see anyone acting suspicious around your locker?" Lizzie asked. "Who was with you when you found it?"

Kate shrugged. "There are always tons of

people hanging around by my locker. I'm super-popular, remember?"

"Right," Lizzie said with a sigh.

Miranda rolled her eyes.

"But I'll tell you one thing," Kate went on. "I think that bubble brain Tammy Jean Honeycutt is the culprit. She's totally jealous of me."

"Maybe . . ." Lizzie said slowly. Tammy Jean did seem to want Kate's cheerleading job. "Is there anybody else?" she asked Kate.

Kate shrugged. "Well, plenty of kids are jealous of me," she said. "But most of them always have been. Tammy Jean is new. And she clearly wants to be head cheerleader."

"Of course, there are other possibilities," Kate continued. "Like those loser geek-boys who ask me out on a daily basis. Especially that repulsive Martin Oglethorpe."

"Has he been bothering you lately?" Miranda asked.

Kate waved as if she were swatting a bug. "I

can't keep track of all the guys who are in love with me. Except maybe Ethan, of course." She smiled sweetly at Lizzie.

Lizzie gritted her teeth. Ethan Craft is my crush-boy, not yours, she thought. Then she remembered why she was there. Stay professional, she told herself. You can do it.

She looked at the note again. All of the *i*'s in the message had cutesy little hearts over them. It didn't seem like something a boy would have written, but it did seem very Tammy Jean.

"I'll see what I can do," she told Kate. "I'll be on the lookout for suspects at the game on Saturday."

When I'm not on the lookout for Ethan, of course!

"Well, thanks," Kate said. She started to leave

the closet, then turned back to face Lizzie and Miranda. "Oh, and ladies?" she added.

"Yes?" Lizzie said.

Kate smiled. "This will be our little secret, okay?" she said as she walked out the door.

Lizzie sighed. Kate will never change, she thought. But a good detective's job is to right wrongs, no matter how obnoxious her client is.

"No wonder someone's trying to make her look bad," Miranda said.

CHAPTER

5

Later that afternoon Lizzie thought about the case as she walked home from school by herself. Gordo was at photography club and Miranda had a dentist appointment.

After school, Lizzie had searched the gym, the girls' locker room, and the cheerleaders' equipment room for clues. But she hadn't come up with anything.

Hmmm, she thought. Who would want to make Kate look bad?

The suspect list could be huge, Lizzie realized.

True, Kate was superpopular. But she had also made a lot of kids at Hillridge supermiserable.

Help! I can't work on this case! I might be a suspect, too!

When Lizzie reached her house, her annoying little brother, Matt, was jumping through hoops in the front yard. Literally.

"Matt, what are you doing?" she asked. She had to dodge three orange-and-green plastic hula hoops to reach the porch steps.

"Heads up, Lizzie!" he called. "I'm coming through!"

Lizzie grabbed her spiky-headed sibling by the T-shirt just as he began another running start. "Don't think so," she said.

"Hey!" a girl's voice shouted. "Let him go. I'm timing him."

Lizzie whirled around. Melina Bianco, the girl Matt wanted to be his girlfriend, was standing by the bushes. She wore a stopwatch around her neck.

"Would somebody please tell me what is going on here?" Lizzie demanded. She looked around at the weird obstacle course set up around the yard. "It doesn't look . . . safe."

Or normal, she thought to herself. But when it comes to Matt, what else is new?

Melina came up to Lizzie and crossed her arms. "For your information," she said, tossing her perfect blond hair, "I am now captain of the Hillridge Elementary cheerleading squad."

Lizzie raised one eyebrow. "You?" she asked Melina. Matt's friend wasn't exactly known for her . . . sunny qualities. She was all business, all the time.

But she is pretty bossy, Lizzie told herself. Sort of like Kate.

"Perhaps you've heard of us," Matt said. "The Little Wildcats?"

Melina turned to Matt. "What do you mean, us? You're not part of the squad yet."

"Whatever you say, my sweet," Matt told her.

Lizzie cringed. The truth was that her little brother was really good at gymnastics. He and his friend Lanny had tried out for cheerleading last year. When there hadn't been room for both boys on the squad, neither of them had joined.

"What about Lanny?" Lizzie asked her brother.

Matt shrugged. "He's got choir rehearsal. So he said it was okay with him."

Melina looked annoyed. She held up her stopwatch. "I don't have all day, you know."

"Right," Matt said. "We'll take it from the top. This time I'll add a triple backflip."

Then he looked at Melina suspiciously. "I am definitely on the squad, right? Guaranteed?"

Melina studied her fingernails. "Well," she

said. "Not exactly. There's no room on the squad at the moment."

Matt's mouth dropped open. "So I'm doing all this for nothing?"

"No," Melina said. "The Little Wildcats mascot is a very important position. I was planning to hold auditions, but if . . ."

"I'll do it!" Matt said eagerly. "You won't regret this, Melina."

The blond girl frowned. "I said *if*," she said. "If you walk, bathe, and groom my dog, plus feed my turtle—and any other pets I may acquire—for the entire football season, I'll put you on the top of the list."

Matt's face fell.

Melina smiled. "There *is* one other way to become the Little Wildcats mascot," she went on.

"Name it, my sugarplum," Matt said eagerly.

"I need your help with a secret mission," Melina said. "In the area of . . ." she lowered her voice, "animal acquisitions."

"Just name the species," Matt told her.

It's amazing what some people will do to impress a big crush. If it were someone like Ethan Craft it would be totally understandable.

"I think I've heard enough," Lizzie said. "Matt, you're on your own."

Lizzie walked into the house, grabbed some chocolate-chip cookies from the kitchen counter, and headed upstairs to her room. She had work to do.

She locked her bedroom door and pulled the detective notebook from under her mattress. Then she made some notes on possible suspects.

Tammy Jean definitely had a motive to make Kate look bad: the head cheerleader job.

But something about that strange, red-haired

girl near the gym door had seemed very suspicious. And she looked so familiar.

Lizzie chewed on her pen. There was a light switch in the hall right outside the gym. The girl could have turned the lights off before Kate's picture came up on the scoreboard.

Hmm, maybe she was working with Tammy Jean.

Lizzie grabbed a Hillridge yearbook from her nightstand. She flipped through the pictures of every single person in their class.

"Zilch," she sighed as she finished the Zs. Then she spotted the red-haired girl—in a picture from last year's football game against their archrival, Jefferson Junior High!

Bingo! We have a positive ID.

The red-haired girl was Reagan Murphy—head of Jefferson's cheer squad!

I have to call Kate, Lizzie told herself. I have to warn her about Reagan!

Rival cheerleaders can be very sneaky. I saw a movie about that once: *Fear to Cheer*.

She reached for the cordless phone next to the bed. Then she punched in Kate's number. She still remembered it from grade school.

Unfortunately, Lizzie got Kate's answering machine. "I'm out doing something more important than you," the recording said. "Leave a message and I'll decide whether to call you back."

"Aargh!" Lizzie said in disgust, slamming down the phone. "Why am I even trying to help that stuck-up snob?"

She'd wait and talk to Kate at school tomorrow. If she felt like it.

The next morning, Tammy Jean was standing by the lockers, greeting everyone. Martin Oglethorpe stood behind her.

"Be sure and take one now," Tammy Jean told Lizzie, Miranda, and Gordo as she held out a basket filled with blue and white rubber bracelets. They had HILLRIDGE SPIRIT! printed on them.

"Do I have to?" Miranda said in a low voice.

"Blue for boys, white for girls," Tammy Jean said, beaming.

"You actually want us to wear these?" Gordo asked. He looked doubtful.

Tammy Jean slipped a blue bracelet on Gordo's wrist. "Why sure, sugar," she said. "Back in Austin, all the students wore spirit bracelets the week of a big game!"

"I have one," Martin put in.

"Well, okay," Gordo said, as he smiled at Tammy Jean. "I guess."

Tammy Jean gave him an extrabig smile. "See? That's the spirit," she said cheerfully.

I bet Gordo ditches that bracelet as soon as we get to our lockers.

Gordo twisted the bracelet around on his wrist. "You know, this is kind of cool," he said.

Just then, Ethan Craft came up behind Lizzie

and her friends. He clapped them all on the backs. Lizzie almost choked on her gum.

"Hey, dudes," he said, holding up his wrist to show his blue bracelet. "I've got one of those, too. Isn't Tammy Jean awesome?"

No, Ethan. *I'm* awesome! *Me*, Lizzie McGuire. ME, ME, ME, ME, ME!!

Instantly, kids started grabbing more bracelets from Tammy Jean's basket. One girl stacked them all the way up her arm.

"I just knew these would be a big hit," Tammy Jean told Martin.

"Well, *I* think they're stupid," Kate said in a loud voice from down the hall. "Don't you, Claire?" She nudged her best friend in the ribs.

Claire frowned at Kate. "No more stupid than you made us look at the pep rally," she said.

Kate's eyes bugged out in shock. "WHAT did you say?" she asked.

Claire shrugged and looked back at the other cheerleaders. They were standing behind her against the lockers.

A few of them looked nervous. But most of them just looked mad.

"We felt like total fools sneezing like that all over the gym," Claire told Kate. "So we took a vote. The squad agreed it's your fault. We don't want you to be head cheerleader anymore."

With that, Claire and the other cheerleaders swept down the hall.

"Oh, wow," Miranda whispered to Lizzie. "This is better than the soaps."

Kate recovered quickly. "Only the head cheer-leader can call for a vote!" she shouted after them. "Besides, only Ms. Bailey can make that decision."

"Oh, I'm sorry, Kate," Tammy Jean said with wide, innocent eyes. She walked over to Kate and patted her gently on the back. "I'm afraid I was the one who called for the vote. I thought that would be more, you know . . . democratic."

For a second, Kate was speechless. Then she practically yelled, "Don't go playing Little Miss Nicey-Nice with me. I know all your tricks. You will never, EVER be head cheerleader at Hillridge. Got it?"

Tammy Jean just smiled.

Then Lizzie noticed something stuck to the back of Kate's expensive cashmere sweater.

It was another note, written in pink sparkle marker. It said:

HI, I'M KATE. KICK ME!

"Um, Kate?" Lizzie said, tapping her on the shoulder.

Kate sighed. "Not now, okay, McGuire?"

"I really need to talk to you," Lizzie insisted. "Like, right now."

She pulled Kate aside and told her about the note.

"Well, get it off me," Kate said.

Lizzie removed the note. It had cutesy little hearts over the *i*'s, just like the first one.

"Tammy Jean," Kate said quietly, narrowing her eyes. "Again."

Lizzie glanced back over her shoulder. Tammy Jean was standing in the center of a group of kids, crying. "I feel so bad," Lizzie heard her sniffle. "I didn't mean to hurt poor Kate, bless her heart. I thought a vote would help her."

"Don't worry, Tammy Jean," one girl said. "We're all behind you."

Kate threw up her hands and began to walk away.

"Wait!" Lizzie said, catching up. "There's something else."

Kate sighed. "Now what?"

Lizzie told her how Reagan Murphy had been at the pep rally.

Kate thought for a minute. "Yeah," she said. "Reagan's definitely up to no good. We've spotted her a few times lately, lurking around our practices."

"Really?" Lizzie asked. She took out a pencil and memo pad to take notes. She'd add them to her detective notebook later.

"In fact," Kate went on, "I saw her sneaking around the bleachers at the football field last week. We had an outdoor practice."

"Do you think Reagan's spying on your routines?" Lizzie asked.

Kate shrugged. "Maybe," she said. "She's probably worried that our squad will show up Jefferson at the regional cheer championship next month."

"That's a motive, all right," Lizzie said, nodding.

"But I still think Tammy Jean is much more dangerous," Kate said. "That slimy snake is the one who's after me, I just know it."

Kate may be right, Lizzie thought. After all, Reagan couldn't have been at Hillridge early enough on the day of the pep rally to leave that first note in Kate's locker.

And Reagan wasn't there today, either. So she couldn't have placed the note on Kate's sweater.

Unless she's working with someone else, Lizzie reminded herself.

Sometimes my own brilliance astounds me.

"Well, there's only one thing to do," Kate said to Lizzie. "You'll have to come to cheerleading practice this afternoon. That way you can keep an eye out for Reagan—and Tammy Jean, of course."

Lizzie gulped. "Umm . . . ME? At cheerleading practice?"

"That's what I said," Kate told her. "Three o'clock sharp. In the gym. Be there."

With that, she strode down the hall.

Lizzie watched her go in dismay. What could be more miserable than cheerleading practice for a girl who didn't make the team last year? she asked herself.

She already knew the answer: not solving this case!

"Gordo would love this," Miranda said to Lizzie. "Even more than the pep rally."

The two of them were sitting in the gym, waiting for cheerleading practice to begin. Miranda was a little grumpy.

"Well, too bad he's at football practice," Lizzie said.

Miranda's eyes widened. "Gordo? At football practice?"

"Yeah, he's asking the guys on the football team some questions before the coach gets there," Lizzie said. "He *is* the Hillridge E-Zine editor, so it's all good."

"What kinds of questions?" Miranda asked.

"He's going to see if they have any idea about who pulled those pranks at the pep rally," Lizzie explained.

Down on the floor, Kate acted as if she were still in charge. She clapped her hands to get the team's attention. "Okay, people, listen up!" she shouted.

None of the cheerleaders paid any attention.

"NOW!" Kate screamed.

Claire and the other cheer queens gathered around her, very slowly. Tammy Jean wasn't there yet.

"They don't seem too happy," Miranda said.

"Would you be?" Lizzie said.

Kate waved toward the bleachers. "Pay no attention to those dorks. They're helping another geek with some article about the big game, so they're observing our practice today."

Miranda turned to Lizzie indignantly. "Did you hear her?" she said. "Are we just going to sit here and take that?"

Lizzie sighed. "We're undercover, remember?"

Miranda crossed her arms and slumped back against the bench. "I'd rather be at football practice. At least then we'd get to watch some cute guys."

"So, okay, let's get started," Kate told the squad. "Where's Ms. Bailey?"

Tammy Jean breezed in the door, waving to everyone. "Hey to y'all, too," she called up to Lizzie and Miranda.

Lizzie wiggled her fingers back. "Just smile," she told Miranda.

Miranda gritted her teeth and smiled.

"You're late," Kate told Tammy Jean.

"I know, and I'm sooo sorry," Tammy Jean gushed. "It's so important to be on time for practice. But I stopped to see Ms. Bailey."

Kate's eyes narrowed. "For what?"

"Oh, we were just visiting," Tammy Jean said. "I told her I have everything under control and we could start practice without her."

"*You* have everything under control? Let's get one thing straight, Tammy Jean Honey Ham—" Kate began.

Tammy Jean looked shocked.

"Kate! That was, like, so rude," one of the girls cut in.

Another girl put her arm around Tammy Jean. "Don't mind Kate. She's just jealous because you're such an awesome cheerleader."

Gordo should film this for a reality TV show. *Cheer Factor*, anyone?

"Oh, I'm sure Kate didn't mean it," Tammy Jean said, trying to smile. "Did you, Kate?"

Kate didn't answer.

"All right then," Tammy Jean went on bravely. "Let's get down to business, shall we? I brought y'all a little present."

She went over to the boom box on the floor and popped in a CD. "This is some really cool music we used back in Austin," she said. "I thought maybe I could show you a few moves from our championship routine."

"No, thanks," Kate said. "We'll be using *our* cheers, the ones we've been rehearsing for months."

Claire frowned. "Why can't we just watch Tammy Jean's routine?"

The other girls started warming up to the beat of the new hip-hop music.

"Here, it goes like this," Tammy Jean said, jumping in front of them. "Two steps left, two steps right—" She began to demonstrate the routine.

Just then, Martin appeared at the back of the

gym. He waved to Tammy Jean, who was still cheering like crazy, and added a few riffs on his tuba.

"Jeesh!" Lizzie said to Miranda, covering her ears. "Does he carry that thing with him everywhere?"

I knew there was a reason I didn't join the marching band.

As the other girls kept cheering, Kate stomped over to Martin. She grabbed the end of his tuba. "Out," she said. "Or I'll stuff YOU with bubbles."

Martin quickly stopped blowing and scowled at Kate. She pointed at the door and stood there watching him until he marched out of the gym indignantly.

Then Kate marched back to the center of the room. "Cut!" she screamed.

But the other girls kept cheering. They actually looked as if they were having fun.

Kate stopped the music. "That stank," Kate said. "We're going back to 'Hold That Line.' Pick up your pom-poms, people."

The cheer queens looked at each other and gathered their pom-poms from a pile near the bleachers.

"We're gonna hold that line, we're gonna stomp our feet," Kate began the cheer.

Behind her, the squad began to wave their pom-poms halfheartedly.

Immediately, the air was filled with blue-and-white confetti.

Caught in the blue-and-white shower, Kate whirled around angrily. "I didn't authorize confetti!" she shouted. "Tammy Jean, you can go get a broom and clean this mess up, pronto."

But Tammy Jean looked confused. "Where did my pom-poms go?"

Lizzie heard Miranda stifle a giggle beside her.

She had to admit, the scene was pretty amusing.

The cheer queens were holding only sticks where the fluffy blue-and-white pom-poms had been. Pom-pom confetti was all over the floor.

"Someone must have shredded them before we got here," Lizzie told Miranda.

The question was, who?

In a fury, Kate grabbed her megaphone. She shouted into it, but nothing came out.

"Uh-oh," Miranda said. "This is gonna be bad."

Kate shouted again.

"Pathetic," Claire said, rolling her eyes. The other girls looked nervous.

Very nervous.

Kate frowned and peered into the end of the megaphone. Then she reached in and pulled out a pair of dirty gym socks.

Pee-ew! I can smell those from here.

Kate quickly dropped the gross socks. A crumpled piece of paper fell to the floor beside them.

"What's that?" Tammy Jean said, rushing forward. Kate tried to grab the paper, but Tammy Jean was too quick for her. She unfolded the note and read it.

Lizzie jumped up, but Kate raised her hand like a traffic cop. "This is strictly a cheerleading matter, McGuire," she said.

Fuming, Lizzie sat down again. "How does Kate expect me to solve the case when I can't even see the clues?" she grumbled to Miranda.

"Shh, this is really getting good," Miranda answered. "Plus, she probably doesn't want people to figure out why you're really here."

"Oh, my," Tammy Jean said, reading the note. She clutched her Aardvarks cheer necklace. "This is terrible."

"Well, what does it say?" Kate demanded.

Tammy Jean shook her head. "I really don't think I should—"

Kate grabbed the note. "It says, 'See you Saturday. If you dare!'" she read.

"Okay, that's it," Claire announced. "We're not going to risk looking like fools in front of the whole school on Saturday. Or at the big cheerleading competition, either. We're out of here."

The other cheerleaders nodded in agreement. They all picked up what was left of their pom-poms and turned to go.

Except for Tammy Jean.

Kate's mouth dropped open. "You mean you're quitting? You can't do that! How dare you?"

"You have forty-eight hours, Sanders," Claire

said over her shoulder. "Clean up this freak show or else."

"If you're not careful, you won't *have* to quit," Kate called. "You'll just be REPLACED!"

"Ha!" Miranda whispered to Lizzie. "This is great! I love cheerleading practice."

"Well, if I don't solve this case soon, there may be some new openings on the squad," Lizzie remarked.

Tammy Jean rushed after the departing cheerleaders. "Wait, y'all!" she cried. "We can work this out. I promise!"

Claire turned around again. "Oh, yeah? How?"

Tammy Jean smiled. "I'll tell you a little secret," she said, leading Claire and the other girls back into the gym. "Something just like this happened back in Austin once. The squad from South Amarillo tried to—"

Just then, Ms. Bailey walked into the gym, her arms full of books and papers. "Sorry, girls," she said. "I'm afraid I got caught up in the faculty room."

What exactly goes on in the faculty room, anyway?

Ms. Bailey looked around and smiled at Tammy Jean. "But I knew you were in good hands after I spoke with Tammy Jean."

"Yeah, this has been a model cheerleading practice all right," Miranda whispered to Lizzie.

"But, Ms. Bailey," Kate began. "All kinds of weird things have been happening ever since Tammy Jean—"

"Yes, I know, Kate," Ms. Bailey said, patting her shoulder. "It's been very difficult lately. Perhaps all the pressure of being head cheerleader is too much."

Kate's eyebrows shot up. "What?"

"Yes, I've been thinking that maybe you could use the help of a *co*-head cheerleader. Someone with good leadership skills—like Tammy Jean," Ms. Bailey suggested.

Tammy Jean blushed. "Who, me?" she asked, sounding surprised.

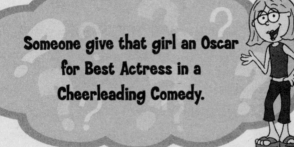

Someone give that girl an Oscar for Best Actress in a Cheerleading Comedy.

"No worries, Ms. Bailey," Kate said quickly. "I can handle everything myself."

"Well, I guess that's okay for now," the cheerleading adviser said slowly. "But I'm sure Tammy Jean would be happy to help."

Tammy Jean nodded eagerly.

"Wow," Miranda said to Lizzie. "Ms. Bailey thinks Tammy Jean is, like, perfect."

"She's perfect, all right," Lizzie said grimly. "The perfect suspect."

Then Lizzie heard a muffled snicker from the hall—and spotted a flash of red hair dashing past the door.

Reagan!

Lizzie jumped up and ran from the bleachers, out of the gym—and smack into a tall, furry wildcat!

Lizzie tried to chase Reagan, but the Wildcats mascot kept blocking her path. Was the person inside the costume doing it on purpose, or was this just a mistake?

"Um, I'm trying to get by," Lizzie said. "Would you mind moving to one side for a minute?"

The mascot stepped to its left and made a slight bow, while gesturing that Lizzie was free to go.

But it was too late. Reagan had vanished down the hall and around a corner.

Lizzie sighed. "Who are you?" she asked the mascot.

The mascot shrugged its shoulders.

So annoying. Matt will make a perfect mascot.

"Did you see a red-headed girl just now?" Lizzie asked. "Was she doing anything weird? Was she in the cheerleaders' equipment room?" She pointed to a door down the hall.

The mascot covered its eyes and ears and shook its head.

"Got it," Lizzie said, rolling her eyes. "Speak no evil, see no evil, hear no evil. Ha-ha."

This mascot, whoever he or she was—was hopeless. But maybe the person in the costume was also Reagan's accomplice.

Lizzie lunged to pull the mascot's head off.

The tall, furry wildcat bolted down the hall, holding its tail.

"Good riddance," Lizzie said.

Since Reagan was long gone, Lizzie decided to check out the cheerleaders' equipment room. It had uniforms, megaphones, and other equipment. It was also used for extra storage by the Hillridge football team, the band, and the drama club.

Luckily, the door was unlocked. Lizzie walked in and almost fell over a pile of boxes. "Guess this is a good place to start," she said aloud.

She began pulling open the boxes. Nothing exciting. New pom-poms—unshredded— traffic cones, a whistle, a first-aid kit, a bunch of reeds and sheet music, gym mats, football helmets.

Lizzie did a quick sweep of the room, but didn't see anything very suspicious. She wasn't exactly sure what she should be looking for.

She decided to try the girls' locker room instead. She walked in and found Kate's and

Tammy Jean's lockers. They were right next to each other.

Kate's was marked HEAD CHEERLEADER. Her picture was pasted on the door. Someone had drawn a mustache on it in pink sparkle marker.

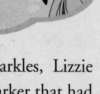

Hmmm . . . an amazing likeness, I'd say.

The culprit sure likes pink sparkles, Lizzie thought. It looked like the same marker that had been used on the two notes.

Tammy Jean wore a lot of pink. On nonspirit days, anyway. A bunch of blue and white balloons and a sign that said WILDCATS 4-EVER!!!! were attached to her locker.

Guess she's gotten over the Aardvarks after all, Lizzie thought.

Suddenly, she spotted a sprinkling of blue-

and-white confetti on the floor—right by Tammy Jean's locker.

The shredded pom-poms, Lizzie told herself. All I need to find now is a pair of scissors.

Lizzie turned around. Sure enough, there was a pair of scissors on the bench right behind her. And a pink sparkle marker.

Hooray for me! Case solved. Now I'm available in case Ethan needs a date for the big dance after the game.

Hmm, Lizzie thought, frowning. There's a whole pile of evidence here. It just seems too obvious.

Tammy Jean was definitely annoying, but was she really that dumb? Lizzie wondered. Anyone who could unglue Kate had to be very smart.

Lizzie picked up the marker and a few pieces of confetti and stuffed them in her pocket, just in case.

Might as well head back to cheerleader practice, she thought with a sigh.

I'll have to deal with Reagan later, Lizzie thought. Right now Tammy Jean has the strongest motive—plus all the evidence points to her.

Things weren't looking good for Ms. Ex-Aardvark.

But why did Reagan keep sneaking around Hillridge?

When Lizzie reached the gym, cheerleading practice was definitely over. Most of the girls had passed Lizzie in the hall, gushing over Tammy Jean.

Miranda was still in the bleachers, blowing huge bubbles with a wad of grape gum. She looked totally bored.

But Tammy Jean was practicing all by herself.

"Be Aggressive! Be-E-Aggressive!" she shouted, jumping up and down.

Kate came up to Lizzie immediately and pulled her aside. It was as if she'd been waiting for her.

"You'd better find the culprit fast, McGuire, or you are T-O-A-S-T," she said. "What kind of detective are you, anyway?"

Lizzie shook herself free. "That's pretty harsh, Kate," she said. "*I'm* the one helping *you* out, remember? I don't know why I even bother."

Kate shrugged. "Yeah, well . . . I guess you're right. Sorry. I'm just a little . . . upset right now." She glanced over her shoulder at Tammy Jean.

Tammy Jean was still cheering. Alone. She was a little too into cheerleading.

Lizzie couldn't help feeling a little sorry for Kate again. "Don't worry, Kate," she said. "I'm about to crack this case, I promise."

"Okay, Sherlock," Miranda said to Lizzie as they left the gym. "Cheerleading practice is finally over. What next? Do you want to meet up with Gordo?"

"No, we can catch up with him later. Let's stop by the athletics office first," Lizzie said. "I want to talk to Mr. Salerno about that scoreboard."

"Well, if you're planning to put our pictures on the scoreboard, you'd better make sure they're better than that photo of Kate at the pep rally," Miranda said.

Yeah. That one ranks right up there with my seventh-grade yearbook photo. Blame the totally uncool unicorn sweater on my mom!

Lizzie knocked on Mr. Salerno's door.

"Come in!" the athletic director called. "And watch your step."

Lizzie nearly tripped over a golf ball rolling past her feet. "Eek!" she cried, jumping out of the way.

"Too bad," Mr. Salerno said. "I missed."

"Excuse me?" Lizzie said.

Mr. Salerno frowned. "I missed the hole," he said. He pointed to a little yellow flag near the door. "I'm practicing my putting and I'm way over par."

"Oh," Lizzie said. "Right. Sorry."

The athletic director put down his golf club.

He looked from Lizzie to Miranda. "So what can I do for you girls?"

"We want to know how to put information up on the gym scoreboard," Lizzie said. "You know, like, special messages. And pictures."

"I'm not authorized to release that information," Mr. Salerno said. "It's classified."

"You mean, like, top secret?" Miranda asked.

Okay, time for the hard-boiled TV detective approach: just hand over the secret 411 and we'll be on our way.

"You need a password to access the scoreboard," Mr. Salerno said. "No one knows it but me."

"Why is it so secret?" Lizzie asked.

Mr. Salerno reached for another golf ball from

a cup on his desk. "There was an unfortunate . . . incident at the pep rally," he said. "Someone cracked the old password to the computer controlling the scoreboard. So I had to change it."

"Was the old password written down somewhere?" Lizzie asked. "Could someone have broken into your office and stolen it?"

Mr. Salerno picked up the putter again. "Nope. My office is locked up tight as Fort Knox. Whoever cracked that code must be some kind of genius."

Hmm, Lizzie thought. Which of my suspects is a genius?

"Now, if you'll excuse me, girls," Mr. Salerno said, "I need to get back to my putting."

We're not going to get anywhere with him, Lizzie thought.

The athletic director was already aiming for the flag.

Lizzie and Miranda quickly left.

"So who do you think cracked the computer

code?" Miranda asked Lizzie as they walked down the hall.

"I'm not sure," Lizzie said. "Tammy Jean may be even smarter than I thought." She sighed. "And I don't know anything about Reagan Murphy."

"Doesn't your old boyfriend Ronny go to Jefferson?" Miranda asked. "Why don't you ask him?"

Okay, Ronny wasn't exactly my boyfriend. But I liked him and he liked me. And we kissed once. That counts, right?

"I guess I could do that," Lizzie said slowly. "I haven't talked to Ronny in a long time, though."

A really, really long time, she thought. He probably doesn't even remember me.

"I think I should go back and check the cheerleaders' room one more time," Lizzie told Miranda. "I keep thinking I missed something big."

Plus, we won't have to talk about Ronny anymore, she added to herself.

The equipment room was still unlocked. Lizzie began to sweep the room for new clues.

"Hey, look!" Miranda called. She took a Hillridge cheerleader uniform from the rack and held it up against her. "What do you think?"

Lizzie grinned. "It's the real you," she said.

"And here's the real you, Elizabeth Brooke McGuire," Miranda said. She pulled a sparkly outfit off a hanger and tossed it to Lizzie.

Lizzie knew she should be doing some serious detective work. But the old Hillridge majorette costume was too tempting.

She pulled it over her T-shirt and jeans and grabbed a rusty baton from a box while Miranda put on the cheerleading uniform.

"Watch this!" Lizzie told Miranda, tossing the

baton in the air. "I got my twirling badge in Girl Scouts."

"Twirling badge?" Miranda snorted. "Yeah, right."

Lizzie totally missed the baton. It bounced off the ceiling and landed at the bottom of the clothes rack. "Oops," she said, embarrassed.

Maybe I should just stick to detective work.

As Lizzie went to retrieve the baton, she brushed against something furry—and warm.

"Gross!" she cried, jumping back.

It was the Hillridge Wildcats mascot uniform, complete with pointy ears and mangy tail. And it definitely reeked.

Miranda held her nose. "Omigosh," she said. "It's that disgusting Team Spirit cologne again!"

Lizzie leaned forward and sniffed the costume.

She almost gagged. "Yep," she said. "That's it. The same stuff someone was wearing at the pep rally."

"It could have been anyone," Miranda said. "That stench carries for miles."

Lizzie frowned. "But now it's coming from the wildcat costume."

Then she remembered who had been sitting in front of them at the pep rally. Who also happened to be very tall. And smart enough to crack a computer password.

Martin Oglethorpe!

But why would he have been wearing the mascot uniform in the hallway?

"We have to find Martin Oglethorpe ASAP," she told Miranda. "I need to ask him some questions."

"Martin?" Miranda said. She wrinkled her nose again. "Do we have to?"

"Yep," Lizzie said. "He's now Official Suspect Number Three."

But as she and Miranda turned to go, Lizzie spied a note taped on a mirror. It said:

3, 5, 7, 9
KATE SANDERS THINKS
SHE'S WAY TOO FINE!

Lizzie examined the message. There were those little hearts over the *i*'s again. The words were kind of smudgy, but the message was clear.

"Kate's right," Lizzie told Miranda. "Someone really is out to make *her* look bad. Not the whole cheer squad."

If you ask me, Kate makes herself look bad 24/7.

"Hey, what's that noise?" Miranda said.

Lizzie listened. There was definitely a rustling somewhere. "Sounds like it's coming from that rack of football jerseys," she said.

She ran over and pushed the uniforms aside. The first thing she saw was a pair of white sneakers. With black-and-red laces.

Jefferson Junior High's colors, Lizzie thought. Then she saw who the sneakers belonged to: Reagan Murphy!

The red-haired girl stood up quickly. "You two are pitiful," she said.

Lizzie and Miranda looked at each other.

"I mean, look at you," Reagan went on. "I can't believe anyone would want to play dress-up in Hillridge uniforms."

Lizzie felt her face turn red. She and Miranda probably did look pretty dumb in their cheer-leader and majorette costumes. But that wasn't the point.

"Listen up, Reagan Murphy," Lizzie said. "I

know who you are. But here's what I want to know: why do you keep sneaking around Hillridge?"

"Yeah," Miranda put in. "We could turn you in to Principal Tweedy for trespassing, you . . . you—"

"Cheerleading spy!" Lizzie finished.

Reagan just laughed. "Oh, puh-leez," she said. "The Hillridge cheer squad is less than pathetic. We already have the cheerleading championship in the bag. Just like every other year. Why bother spying?"

She does have a point, Lizzie thought. But still . . .

"Maybe you two should look for the person who's freaking out Kate Sanders in your own school," Reagan added. She headed toward the door.

"Hey, come back here!" Lizzie called. "What's that supposed to mean?"

"Yeah," Miranda said. "And if you're not a spy,

then why are you hiding in the equipment room?"

"That," Reagan said, "is for me to know and you to find out. But right now, I have a *real* cheerleading practice to attend. Good luck, geeks."

With a wave at Lizzie and Miranda, she walked out.

Wow, being supersnobby must be a requirement for head cheerleaders.

Gordo caught up with Lizzie and Miranda as they left school. "Hey, Lizzie, I have some info for you!" he said.

"Good," Lizzie said. "We definitely need a break in this case."

"Well, I didn't learn a whole lot about the

sneezing powder or the scoreboard prank," Gordo said, "but a couple of players told me that this girl from Jefferson has been hanging around Hillridge a lot."

"Would that girl's name happen to be . . . Reagan Murphy?" Miranda pretended to guess.

Gordo looked disappointed. "Yeah," he said. "How did you know?"

"Oh, we have our ways, Gordo," Miranda said.

I'm definitely going to have to get the scoop on Reagan, Lizzie thought. I'll call Ronny tonight. Maybe.

But Lizzie didn't say that out loud. Not that Gordo would care or anything.

When Lizzie and her friends reached the McGuires' house, they found Matt hard at work.

Dressed as a mini–Wildcat mascot, he was jumping and flipping and tumbling all over the yard.

Melina tapped a spirit stick against one hand.

"You call that a reverse double backflip?" she snorted. "Ha!"

"Wow," Miranda whispered to Lizzie and Gordo. "She actually makes Kate look nice."

"Again!" Melina called. "Twice as fast, please."

Matt redoubled his gymnastics efforts. But Melina was still unimpressed.

Watching her little brother, Lizzie remembered that other Wildcat mascot—the tall, smelly one.

Martin was definitely a suspect in the Kate Hater mystery. But was he the culprit?

"Come on, guys," she told Miranda and Gordo. "Let's go inside."

In the kitchen, Lizzie scooped some ice cream and presented her case against Martin.

"He definitely has a motive," Lizzie said. "Kate turned him down. *And* she had the guys from the football team turn his tuba into a bubble machine."

"Yeah, that might make a guy a little mad," Gordo said.

"Martin's also smart enough to crack a computer code," Lizzie went on.

"And he's got a mongo crush on Tammy Jean," Miranda added. "He'd do anything for that girl."

"Well, she is very nice," Gordo said.

Lizzie and Miranda looked at each other. "Anyway," Lizzie said, "maybe he wants to make Kate look stupid in front of everyone to impress Tammy Jean," Lizzie said.

Then she thought of something else. She froze, her spoon of ice cream in midair. "Hey, what if Martin wants to get rid of Kate as head cheerleader so Tammy Jean can grab the job?"

"Whoa," Gordo said. "A very impressive deduction, Detective McGuire."

Thank you, my dear colleague, Gordo. Now, if I could only apply those brilliant deductive reasoning skills to geometry class.

Lizzie twirled her spoon. "Martin and Tammy Jean could even be working together," she said.

"No doubt about it, Lizzie," Miranda said. "You're definitely onto something."

"Maybe," she said. "But what are we going to do about it?"

"Okay, I have a plan," Lizzie told Miranda and Gordo half an hour later.

"Good," said Gordo. "Because we've finished all the ice cream and a whole box of cookies."

"And the pretzels," Miranda said, popping the last one in her mouth.

All this detective work requires extra snacking. Preferably of the junk-food variety!

"So what's the plan?" Gordo said.

"We're all going undercover at the game on Saturday—even Matt," Lizzie said.

"Undercover?" Miranda asked suspiciously. "For the record, I am not posing as a cheerleader."

"Me neither," Gordo joked.

"Would I do that to my best friends?" Lizzie said innocently. "Just follow me."

She walked out into the yard.

Mini-Wildcat Matt was still being put through his paces by Melina. "It's hopeless," Melina told him. "You will fail on your secret mission."

"Never, my darling," Matt said, twirling his cat whiskers.

"I have a deal for you, Melina," Lizzie announced.

Melina looked wary. "What kind of deal?"

Lizzie put an arm around Melina's shoulders. "Miranda and I happen to be very tight with the

Hillridge Junior High Wildcats cheerleaders."

"We do?" Miranda asked. Lizzie nudged her to be quiet.

"That's right," Lizzie went on. "In fact, I bet we could get the Little Wildcats squad on the field to help cheer in the Jefferson game on Saturday," Lizzie said.

Melina's mouth dropped open. "Really?"

I'm going to owe Kate big-time for this. Hey, waitie just a sec—*she'll* owe *me* for solving the case!

"There's just one thing," Lizzie continued, "Matt has to be there, too."

Now it was Matt's turn to look surprised.

"What's in it for you?" Melina asked Lizzie.

Lizzie patted Matt on his spiky head. "I just

want to help my wonderful little brother and his friends," she said sweetly.

"Hmm," Melina said, thinking it over. "Well, it does put me and Matt in an even better position for our secret mission," she said.

What is she talking about? Lizzie wondered. On the other hand, I don't think I want to know.

"Okay," Melina told Lizzie finally. "It's a deal." She turned to Matt. "I'm going home to finalize plans. Keep practicing."

"Okay, sister dearest," Matt said, as soon as Melina left the yard. "What do you want?"

Lizzie smiled. "I need you to do a little job for me—in return for giving your girlfriend her big chance to dazzle the junior high cheerleaders at the game."

Matt sighed. "Yeah, yeah. What is it?"

"Just a bit of undercover work while you're wearing your Wildcat costume. I want you to keep an eye out for any suspicious persons or behavior. In particular, the junior high mascot."

"I have no clue what you're talking about," Matt said. "But okay."

He went back to work on his gymnastics routine.

"You know, Lizzie," Gordo said. "I've never actually seen the Hillridge Wildcats mascot at any games this season."

"Unless you count Hilly," Miranda put in.

"Who's Hilly?" Lizzie asked.

"It's a big, orange-striped cat that belongs to the football coach's wife," Miranda said.

"Oh, yeah," Gordo said. "She brings that cat to the games in a carrier. Right before the coin toss, she holds him up to the crowd for good luck."

A lucky kitty? Give me a break. On the other hand, Hillridge is undefeated this season!

"Whatever," Lizzie said. "But I have a feeling our mascot will show up this time. And underneath that costume we'll find a very sneaky geek."

The next day at school, Lizzie pulled Gordo and Miranda aside in the library. "Will you guys go with me to Jefferson Junior High this afternoon?"

"You didn't call Ronny, did you?" Miranda asked.

"Um, no," Lizzie said.

"Ronny who?" Gordo asked, puzzled.

"Never mind," Lizzie said. She gave Miranda a warning look.

"Chicken," Miranda whispered.

So what if I didn't have the guts to talk to Ronny, Lizzie thought.

"We need to officially rule out Reagan as a suspect," Lizzie said. "I checked Jefferson's football schedule on the Internet. They have a home game against Glenview this afternoon."

"So you want to spy on the spy?" Miranda asked.

"Exactly," Lizzie said.

"Well, I'm in," Miranda said.

"Me, too," Gordo said. "I guess I can skip photography club. Larry Tudgeman's going to show his pictures from the Intergalactic Society convention."

Now, that is one event I would really hate to miss. Not.

After school, Lizzie and her friends rode the bus to Jefferson, the next town over. They got to the game just as it was starting.

"Reagan wasn't lying about one thing," Lizzie said. "The Jefferson cheer squad is way better than ours."

"Yeah," Miranda said. "She doesn't have any reason to spy on Kate."

"And she couldn't have taped the 'Kick Me' note to Kate's sweater," Lizzie added. "That was at the beginning of the school day."

"Unless she was working with someone from Hillridge," Gordo pointed out.

"Yeah, but Reagan still has no motive," Lizzie said.

"Maybe she's not checking out the cheerleaders," Gordo said. "She could be checking out our football team."

Lizzie and Miranda both stared at him.

"For strategy," Gordo added quickly. "We've been winning all our games, right? Maybe Reagan is spying for Jefferson."

Just then, a cute blond guy stood up in the stands a few rows away. "Hey, Lizzie!" he called.

Lizzie looked over. "Omigosh, it's Ronny!" she whispered to Miranda. "What should I do?"

"Go talk to him," Miranda suggested.

Lizzie frowned. "He has a girl with him," she said. "It's probably his girlfriend. And she doesn't look very happy."

Then she heard Ronny tell the girl, "Don't get all mad, Stacy. She's just a girl on my paper route who goes to Hillridge."

Lizzie's face flamed. What a jerk, she thought. He could at least mention I was his girlfriend once.

Okay, so it was for a nanosecond. But it totally happened!

Kids around Ronny overheard him. "Hey, she's from Hillridge?" someone said loudly.

"Yeah, what's she doing here?" someone else complained.

"She's got a notebook," a girl behind Lizzie

said. She leaned forward. "Are you taking notes on our plays?"

Lizzie gulped. I can't say it's my detective notebook, she thought.

"Hey, what's going on?" Gordo asked, looking up from his camera, which still didn't seem to be working.

"He's taking pictures!" a guy shouted.

Kids began to yell and throw food at Lizzie and her friends.

"Uh-oh," Miranda said, defending herself against a shower of fries. "This crowd's getting ugly."

"Let's get out of here," Lizzie said.

"Good plan," Gordo agreed. "But how?"

Just then, Reagan stepped forward from the cheerleaders' bench. "It's okay," she said through her megaphone. "They're friends of mine."

To Lizzie's shock, Reagan waved the three of them down to the field.

"Why is Reagan being nice to us?" Miranda

asked as they started down the bleachers.

"I have no idea," Lizzie said. "But let's just go with it. Anything to escape the flying fries."

"You guys shouldn't be here," Reagan hissed when Lizzie and her friends got to the field. "There's a path that way, out the back. Now beat it!"

She nodded toward a long line of tall bushes. A narrow dirt path cut through the middle of the bushes and led to the street.

"I can't believe she actually helped us," Miranda said, when she, Lizzie, and Gordo were safely on the path.

"Well, I can," Lizzie said. "There's the reason."

She pointed to a spot in the bushes just ahead of them. The Hillridge Junior High quarterback, Steve Ramos, was hiding there—holding a bunch of flowers!

"You're waiting for Reagan Murphy, aren't you?" Lizzie asked.

Steve's face turned bright red. "No," he said.

"Well, okay, yes. I wanted to surprise her when she finishes cheering. Look, don't tell anyone, okay?" Steve said. "It's just a little game Reagan and I play. We hide and surprise each other all the time."

"Huh?" Miranda said. "That's the dumbest thing I ever heard."

I think it's totally romantic—like Romeo and Juliet. Our schools are archrivals and they don't want anyone to discover their secret love. Sigh.

"Let's go, guys," Gordo said. He glanced over his shoulder. "I think some football players are coming to escort us out."

The Hillridge quarterback dove into the bushes.

Lizzie, Miranda, and Gordo ran for the bus.

"Well, I guess now we know the reason Reagan was sneaking around Hillridge," Lizzie said, when they were finally on their way home. "That's why she was at our pep rally and hiding in the cheerleaders' room."

"I still think that hiding deal is the stupidest thing I ever heard," Miranda said. Gordo was absorbed with his broken camera again.

"At least we can cross Reagan off our suspect list," Lizzie said. "So that leaves two: Martin the Super Dweeb and Ms. Ex-Texas."

"I think it's time to have a heart-to-heart with Tammy Jean," Lizzie said to Miranda and Gordo as they rode the bus home. "Like, right now."

"Okay," Miranda said. "Where does she live?"

"She rides our bus, remember?" Lizzie said. "Tammy Jean lives on Sunnyside Avenue. We should just get off one stop earlier."

"Even her street is cheerful," Miranda muttered.

"Do you mind if I catch up with you two later?" Gordo asked. "I need to stop at the camera store and get this looked at before the game."

"Sure, Gordo," Lizzie said. "No prob."

I guess he's not that in love with Tammy Jean after all.

Luckily, Tammy Jean was at home. She answered the door in a pink bathrobe and fuzzy slippers. Her hair was in curlers, and her eyes were puffy as if she'd been crying.

"Omigosh!" Lizzie said. "Tammy Jean, are you okay?"

"Yeah, you look awful," Miranda said.

Lizzie poked her friend.

"I am soooo glad to see you two," Tammy Jean said, inviting them in. She gave both girls a big, weepy hug.

"Maybe we should sit down somewhere," Lizzie said.

Tammy Jean blew her nose. "Sure," she said.

She led Lizzie and Miranda to the living room and plopped into an overstuffed armchair. "You know my dad's a big oil executive, right?" she said, sniffing.

"Um, no," Lizzie said.

"Well, anyway, his company just changed their minds about Hillridge. Now they're transferring him to Alaska."

"Great! You're going to move!" Miranda said.

Sometimes Miranda is just a little too . . . honest.

Lizzie threw her a warning look.

"I mean, gee, that's terrible," Miranda corrected.

"We're leaving in only a month," Tammy Jean sobbed. "Before the regional cheerleading championships!"

"That's too bad," Lizzie said. "I know you were looking forward to those."

Tammy Jean nodded. "And that's not all. I went online and found out my new school doesn't even *have* a cheerleading squad."

"Horrors," Miranda said.

Tammy Jean reached for another tissue on the coffee table. "I hate moving around so much. That's one of the reasons I love cheerleading." She looked from Lizzie to Miranda. "I get a built-in circle of new friends."

"Well, don't feel bad," Miranda said. "Maybe you can take up snowshoeing. Or, hey, how about ice hockey? You know: Be-E Aggressive!"

"You'll do great in Alaska, Tammy Jean," Lizzie said quickly. "You're such an . . . enthusiastic person. Just look at all the friends you've made at Hillridge already."

"Not Kate Sanders," Tammy Jean said glumly.

"No, no," Lizzie lied. "She thinks you're the most . . . highly motivated cheerleader ever."

In other words, she hates your guts!

Tammy Jean brightened a bit. "Really?" she said. Then she shrugged. "Well, at least I won't have to deal with that pest Martin Oglethorpe anymore."

Lizzie raised an eyebrow at Miranda.

"He told me the whole sad story of how Kate turned down his affections," Tammy Jean went on. "I felt really sorry for him, so I tried to be nice. But then he went overboard."

Lizzie leaned forward. "What did he do, Tammy Jean?"

"He told me he'd help me become head cheerleader at Hillridge," Tammy Jean said. "He never said how. I just hope he wasn't responsible for any of those pranks on Kate.

"The worst part is," Tammy Jean continued, "I'm allergic to him. Like, for real. It must be that horrible cologne he started wearing. I think he was trying to impress me."

Hmmm, Lizzie thought, as Miranda stifled a gag. Horrible cologne? That's got to be Team Spirit, which means he was definitely the person wearing the Wildcat costume. But why?

Now that Tammy Jean and Reagan are both out of the picture, Martin has to be the culprit, Lizzie thought.

"I'm sorry, Tammy Jean, but we have to go," Lizzie said, standing up. She handed the girl the whole box of tissues. "We'll see you at the big game tomorrow, okay?"

"Sure," Tammy Jean said. "The show must go on, right?" She smiled bravely. "Thank you for stopping by. You're true friends."

"We've got to go to Kate's house," Lizzie told

Miranda as they hurried away. "I have to tell her that the mystery is solved—and warn her about Martin."

Kate answered the door. But she wasn't exactly thrilled to see Lizzie and Miranda.

"I can't talk right now," Kate told them. "I'm getting ready for a big date."

Some date, Lizzie thought. Kate was wearing sweats. And she had some kind of weird pink goo on her fingernails.

"But, Kate," Lizzie said. "I really think you need to know—"

"See you tomorrow," Kate said, waggling her fingers. "Buh-bye." She practically slammed the door in their faces.

"That was so rude," Lizzie said.

"That was so Kate," Miranda corrected. "What did you expect?"

"I didn't even have a chance to tell her I solved the case," Lizzie said. "Or about Martin, or Reagan, or Tammy Jean moving."

"If you ask me," Miranda said, "I think you should let Martin go ahead with whatever dirty trick he's planning for the game tomorrow."

"That is very tempting," Lizzie admitted. "But I gave Kate my word. And if Martin's the culprit, he's just as bad as she is."

"True," Miranda said.

"We still don't have hard evidence on Martin," Lizzie said. "And no matter what a pain Kate is, I'm a professional detective. Justice must be served, right?"

"If you say so," Miranda said.

"Well, here we are," Miranda said to Lizzie. "It's game day."

Lizzie looked around the football field. The Hillridge bleachers were packed. So was the Jefferson section.

Lizzie scanned the crowd.

She spotted Gordo on the sidelines, taking pictures. He gave Lizzie a wave.

The Hillridge cheerleaders were trying to rev their side up. Kate and Tammy Jean were trying to outshout each other, as usual.

The Little Wildcats were right near them.

The Jefferson cheerleaders were cheering, too. They were definitely louder than the Hillridge squad.

Reagan Murphy kept looking over her shoulder at Steve Ramos and batting her eyelashes.

The Hillridge quarterback waggled his fingers, as if he were warming them up.

That's hilarious, Lizzie thought. He's actually waving to Reagan!

Then Steve got sacked by a Jefferson linebacker before he even threw the ball.

The Hillridge crowd booed. "Ouch," Lizzie muttered.

She looked around again. Where was Matt?

Almost on cue, her brother ran out onto the field in front of the Wildcats' bench. He did a few flips and fell flat on his cat nose.

Lizzie frowned. Her little brother was annoying, all right. But he never missed flips.

Matt tripped over his own tail and rolled toward the Hillridge team bench.

"Hey!" said one of the football players. "Get this thing out of here." He gave Mini-Wildcat Matt a nudge with one cleat.

Matt stood up and clumsily knocked over an entire cooler of Gatorade. It splashed all over Kate and Tammy Jean and the rest of the Hillridge cheerleaders.

"Excellent," said Miranda.

"Omigosh," Lizzie said. "What is he doing *now*?"

He has to be the worst mascot ever!

Matt took a running start toward the coach's wife, who was sitting in the first row. Hilly the lucky cat was in his carrier at her feet.

With a jaw-dropping, double somersault–backflip combination, Matt swooped down and picked up the carrier. Then he raced down the field.

The coach's wife stood up and screamed. Her husband waved his arms at the referee. "Stop the game!" he called.

Aha, Lizzie thought. So THAT was Matt and Melina's secret mission: catnapping poor Hilly for Melina's ever-growing pet collection!

If cats have nine lives, Hilly better hope he doesn't have to spend too many of them with Melina. MeeeOW!

Unfortunately for Matt, the Hillridge coach ordered the whole team to go after him. The players caught up to Matt and tackled him.

The cat carrier went flying, but luckily a wide receiver was there to catch it.

Melina disappeared into the crowd.

"Your brother's going to have a lot of explaining to do, Lizzie," Miranda said.

"Serves him right," Lizzie said. The Hillridge football players were dragging Matt back by the tail.

Lizzie suddenly spotted Martin in the bleachers. But he wasn't wearing the mascot costume. He was wearing his band uniform—and playing the tuba with the rest of the band!

I wonder what he's up to, Lizzie thought.

"I'll be right back," Lizzie told Miranda. "I'm going to question Martin. Maybe I can get him to crack before he does anything."

"I'm going with you," Miranda said.

"No," Lizzie told her. "You stay here and help the Little Wildcats."

"*Me*?" Miranda said, gulping. All the grade-school cheerleaders were smiling at her expectantly.

"You'll do great," Lizzie said as she hurried toward the bleachers. Behind her, she heard Miranda say, "Okay, Little Wildcats, listen up. We're gonna do high kicks—to the Hillridge fight song!"

"Yay!" the young cheerleaders said excitedly. "You're the best! That's our favorite!"

Lizzie grinned as she ran up the bleachers. Miranda's a total pro, she told herself. Martin stopped playing his tuba when he saw Lizzie standing in front of him with her arms crossed.

"Tammy Jean told me what you said," Lizzie began.

"Okay, okay," he said. "I confess. I did it."

Huh? My suspect crumbles just like that? That's not the way it's supposed to work. I was just warming up!

"I wanted to impress Tammy Jean and help her become head cheerleader by making Kate look bad. It was a terrible mistake."

"Um, right," Lizzie said. "Go on." This is way too easy, she thought.

"I shook sneezing powder in Kate's pom-poms before the pep rally," Martin went on. "But I spilled the bottle by mistake, and it got all over everyone else's, too."

He looked down at his tuba sadly. "Now Tammy Jean sneezes every time she comes near me," he said.

It's not the sneezing powder, Lizzie told him silently.

Martin looked as if he were about to cry. "I put that message and Kate's picture on the scoreboard. I even cracked the secret password to get access. But Tammy Jean thought that was really mean. I think she suspects I did it, even though she's too nice to say anything. You won't rat, will you, Lizzie?"

This guy is totally losing it, Lizzie thought. "It depends," she answered. "What about all the other stuff you did?"

Martin looked confused. "What other stuff?" he said. "The sneezing powder and the scoreboard were disastrous enough. I didn't do anything else."

"Then what were you doing in that Wildcats costume outside the gym?" Lizzie asked.

Martin shrugged. "I wanted to watch Tammy Jean practice after Kate kicked me out," he said. "I needed a costume."

"And what about all the notes? And the pom-pom confetti?" Lizzie asked.

"Huh?" Martin asked.

Just then, the crowd began to cheer. The game was starting again.

Lizzie turned around.

Down on the field, Kate began to lead a cheer. She leaped into the air in a half-decent split jump.

Not bad, Lizzie thought.

Then she noticed something strange.

There was some kind of pink stuff on the bottom of Kate's sneakers. It looked like the same weird goo she had on her hands the night before.

Lizzie frowned. What *is* that stuff? she wondered.

"I'll talk to you later," Lizzie said to Martin. She headed back down the bleachers.

Suddenly, Kate dropped to the ground, screaming. "My ankle!" she cried.

Ms. Bailey and the Hillridge team trainer ran toward Kate.

Tammy Jean stopped cheering and rushed over, too.

Wincing in pain, Kate pointed to the bottom of her sneakers. "Someone put this slimy goo on them to make me trip," she said. "On purpose!"

"Take it easy, now, young lady," the trainer said. "We'll check that ankle out right away."

"I think I'd better go to the locker room instead," Kate suggested.

Kate got up and started bossing people around on her way to the locker room. Guess she isn't in too much pain, Lizzie thought.

Waitie just a sec. . . .

I know exactly who the culprit is, Lizzie thought. But I don't have much time!

Lizzie ran ahead of everyone else to the locker room. Just as she'd suspected, one of the lockers was wide open.

A large bottle of pink Silly Goop was sitting on the shelf of Tammy Jean's cubby.

"Aha!" Lizzie said. She grabbed the bottle and stuck it in her backpack, just as Kate hobbled into the locker room.

Ms. Bailey, the trainer, Miranda, and the whole Hillridge cheer squad were right behind her.

Kate's eyes flashed to Tammy Jean's locker. Then they narrowed into little green slits as she looked at Lizzie. "What are you doing, McGuire?" she hissed.

Lizzie shrugged. "My job," she said quietly. "I've solved the case. And I think everyone's going to be very . . . surprised."

A funny look came over Kate's face. "Okay, people," she called. "My ankle's feeling much better now, thanks. I must have stepped in some gum, that's all. You can go now. Tammy Jean, you're in charge. Get the game started again."

Tammy Jean seemed doubtful. "Are you sure, Kate?"

Kate rolled her eyes. "I'm sure. Now get out!"

Everyone hurried away except Miranda.

"You're not as good a detective as I thought, McGuire," Kate said. "You can't have solved the case. You missed a major clue in here."

Lizzie looked straight at Kate. "Oh, I've solved the mystery, all right. Really classy, Kate, attempting to frame Tammy Jean."

Kate studied her perfectly manicured nails. They still had a faint ring of pink around them from the night before, Lizzie noticed. From when she applied that goop to her sneakers. "I don't know what you're talking about," she said.

"After Martin ruined the pep rally, you got the idea to do all those other mean things to yourself," Lizzie said. "That first crumpled note, the shredded pom-poms, the socks in the megaphone—"

"Can we discuss this later?" Kate asked. "My ankle is hurting again."

Lizzie began to pace in front of the lockers. "You had a very strong motive, too. You wanted

Tammy Jean to get kicked off the squad. That way she'd never become co–head cheerleader."

"You're a liar, McGuire," Kate said.

"I don't think so," Lizzie answered. She turned and left the locker room, dragging Miranda with her.

Was that a lousy dramatic exit or what? Why can't I ever come up with a good parting line?

Miranda was speechless.

Gordo came running up. "What happened in there?" he asked.

Lizzie told him the whole story.

"Amazing," Gordo said, shaking his head.

Miranda finally snapped out of her haze. "Why didn't you tell Ms. Bailey what happened?" she said. "Or someone?"

Lizzie sighed. "I didn't want to be a rat," she

said, "like Kate. Besides, Kate didn't hurt anyone but herself."

"Yeah," Gordo added. "I bet knowing Lizzie figured out the truth is enough punishment for her."

The three of them walked back toward the game.

"You'd think Kate could have at least apologized to you for wasting all that time," Miranda grumbled.

"Well, it wasn't a total waste of time," Lizzie said. "I think we all learned a valuable lesson here."

"Once a cheer beast, always a cheer beast?" Miranda asked as Kate stomped past them on her miraculously healed ankle.

"No," Lizzie said. "More like, sometimes things just aren't what they seem."

"I can't believe Kate's going back out there," Gordo said.

"She's *Kate*, Gordo," Miranda said. "What do you expect?"

Lizzie and her friends took seats in the bleachers. Hillridge was winning, 14-7.

"So what's our next cheer, captain?" Tammy Jean asked Kate. The rest of the cheer queens were waiting expectantly.

Kate glanced over at Lizzie. "You can lead, Tammy Jean," she said.

Tammy Jean beamed. "Really?" she squealed. "Gee, thanks, Kate. You're the best! Come on, Wildcats cheerleaders. Got the spirit? Let's hear it!"

She's going to do just fine in Alaska.

"Another case solved," Lizzie said to Miranda. "Now, let's move on to the next mystery. Where's Ethan?"

Want to have a way-cool time? Here's a clue. . . . Read the next Lizzie McGuire mystery!

Spring It On!

Spring has sprung at Hillridge Junior High, and that brings two things: the big Spring Fling dance and spring showers. While the unending rain depresses Lizzie, Miranda is totally psyched. Her theme for this year's Spring Fling dance (Flower Power!) has been chosen over a ton of other ideas. Now Miranda is in charge of the whole thing— and she's drafted Lizzie to help. Unfortunately, disasters begin to "spring" up as Miranda and Lizzie prepare the gym for the dance, and Lizzie suspects foul play. Can she track down the spring sneak before her best friend's big night is ruined?

My clues are not all wet— I just need an umbrella.